From an episode of the animated TV series *Franklin*,
produced by Nelvana Limited, Neurones France s.a.r.l. and
Neurones Luxembourg S.A, based on the Franklin books
by Paulette Bourgeois and Brenda Clark.

NELVANA   NEURONES

Story written by Sharon Jennings.

Illustrated by Sasha McIntyre, Robert Penman and Shelley Southern.

Based on the TV episode *Franklin's Pond Phantom*, written by Brian Lasenby.

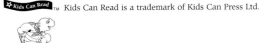 Kids Can Read is a trademark of Kids Can Press Ltd.

Franklin

Franklin is a trademark of Kids Can Press Ltd.
The character of Franklin was created by Paulette Bourgeois and Brenda Clark.
Text © 2005 Contextx Inc.
Illustrations © 2005 Brenda Clark Illustrator Inc.

Kids Can Press acknowledges the financial support of the Government of Ontario,
through the Ontario Media Development Corporation's Ontario Book Initiative; the
Ontario Arts Council; the Canada Council for the Arts; and the Government of
Canada, through the BPIDP, for our publishing activity.

Published in Canada by
Kids Can Press Ltd.
29 Birch Avenue
Toronto, ON M4V 1E2

Published in the U.S. by
Kids Can Press Ltd.
2250 Military Road
Tonawanda, NY 14150

www.kidscanpress.com

Series editor: Tara Walker
Edited by Jennifer Stokes
Designed by Céleste Gagnon

Printed and bound in China by WKT Company Limited

The hardcover edition of this book is smyth sewn casebound.
The paperback edition of this book is limp sewn with a drawn-on cover.

CM 05 0 9 8 7 6 5 4 3 2 1
CM PA 05 0 9 8 7 6 5 4 3 2 1

Library and Archives Canada Cataloguing in Publication

Jennings, Sharon
      Franklin's pond phantom / Sharon Jennings ;
illustrated by Sasha McIntyre, Robert Penman, Shelley Southern.

(Kids Can read)
The character Franklin was created by Paulette Bourgeois and Brenda Clark.
ISBN 1-55337-718-4 (bound). ISBN 1-55337-719-2 (pbk.)

I. McIntyre, Sasha II. Penman, Robert (Robert David)
III. Southern, Shelley IV. Bourgeois, Paulette V. Clark, Brenda VI. Title.
VII. Series: Kids Can read (Toronto, Ont.)

PS8569.E563F7173 2005   jC813'.54   C2004-904711-6

Kids Can Press is a *lorus*™ Entertainment company

1656

Franklin's Pond Phantom

Kids Can Press

Franklin can tie his shoes.

Franklin can count by twos.

And Franklin can hardly

wait to go looking for

the Pond Phantom.

He read about the phantom in a book.

So Franklin knows it *must* be real.

Franklin ran to find his parents.

"I am going to look for

the Pond Phantom," he said.

"It lives deep, deep down

in Woodland Pond."

"But no one has
seen the phantom
for a long, long time,"
said his father.

"Well, *I'm* going to see

it today," said Franklin.

"Be home for supper,"

said his mother.

Franklin went to the pond.

"I will watch and wait," he said.

"I *know* I will see

the Pond Phantom."

Franklin sat down.

He watched

and waited.

He waited

and watched.

Soon, he

fell asleep.

In a little while, Franklin woke up.

The sun was shining.

The water sparkled.

The air was hazy.

And something tall and white

was moving across the water.

Franklin rubbed his eyes.

"It's the Pond Phantom!" he shouted.

Franklin ran to tell his friends.

"I saw the Pond Phantom!" he cried.

"Wow!" said Bear.

"My great-granny

saw it once."

"Well, I've never seen it,"

said Beaver.

"And I live *in* the pond."

"Let's go to the pond now," said Franklin.

"Maybe we can all see the Pond Phantom."

Franklin and Bear and Beaver

went to the pond.

"I was sitting right here," said Franklin.

"And I saw a big, white monster!"

"Ooooh," said Bear.

"And it was heading straight for me,"

added Franklin.

"Hmph!" said Beaver.

Everyone watched and waited.

Nothing happened.

"I think the phantom

is a phony,"

said Beaver.

"I'm going home."

"Me too," said Bear.

"I'm hungry."

Soon, Franklin had an idea. "A photo will show the phantom's not a phony," he said.

He ran home for his camera.

He ran back to the pond.

The sun was shining.

The water sparkled.

The air was hazy.

And something tall and white

was moving across the water!

SNAP!

Franklin took a photo of the phantom!

Franklin ran to the store.

His photo was printed.

It was a little blurry.

But the photo showed something

tall and white moving across the water.

"Wow!" said Franklin.

"I *did* see the Pond Phantom!"

The next day, Franklin met

Bear and Beaver at the pond.

Franklin held out the photo.

"Wow!" said Bear.

Beaver grabbed the photo.

"This looks like a big, white

blur to me," she said.

"I want to see the Pond Phantom

for myself!"

So Franklin and Bear and Beaver sat down.

They watched and waited.

They waited
and watched.

Soon, Bear and

Beaver fell asleep.

Franklin went for a walk
around the pond.
He saw Mr. Mole and
showed him the photo.
"Wow!" said Mr. Mole.
"No one has seen the
Pond Phantom in years!"

Then Mr. Mole had a good idea.

"Let's get in my boat and look

for the phantom," he said.

Franklin and Mr. Mole walked

to the dock.

They got into the boat.

It had a tall, white sail.

Franklin and Mr. Mole sailed

all around the pond.

They did not see the Pond Phantom.

Back on the shore,

Bear and Beaver woke up.

The sun was shining.

The water sparkled.

The air was hazy.

And something tall and white

was moving across the water!

"Look!" said Bear.

"The Pond Phantom

is coming right at us!"

"Listen!"

said Beaver.

"The Pond Phantom

is calling our names!"

The Pond Phantom came closer

and closer until ...

… it came right

up to the shore.

Out jumped Franklin.

Mr. Mole sailed away.

"We went looking for

the Pond Phantom," said Franklin.

"But we didn't see it anywhere."

"Well, *we* did," said Beaver.

"Really?" asked Franklin. "Where?"

"Turn around and look," said Bear.

Franklin turned around and looked.

The sun was shining.

The water sparkled.

The air was hazy.

And something tall and white
was moving across the water!

"It's the Pond Phantom!" cried Franklin.

Bear and Beaver laughed.

"It is *not* the Pond Phantom," said Beaver.

"It is just Mr. Mole's boat," said Bear.

"What?!" said Franklin.

He turned and looked again.

He looked.

And he looked.

"Phooey," he said.

He waved to Mr. Mole.

"Let's go home," said Franklin.

"I guess the phantom is
a phony after all."